The Smallest of Entryways

The Smallest of Entryways

Short Stories

by

Cristen Hemingway Jaynes

There are two candles;
one in the window, for hope,
the other lit for mourning.

CONTENTS

The Lamp

The drizzle covered the city in a stovepipe mist, tinting the grey concrete of the roads and buildings a bluish color. The father drove the old brown Rover that was new to him with the steady uncertainty of training a new horse. It was two o'clock, the first time he had come to the house since he'd moved out. He was there to pick up his daughter. The neighborhood was always quiet, its residents mostly old couples and widowed old women. The young couple and their daughter had ended up there thanks to the funeral home which they had lived above before buying the house. A few times the owner of the funeral home had asked the father to work for him, and though he had always said, "No, I have a job; thank you anyway," he had, a number of times, helped the owner if the owner found him at home. Sometimes the owner would knock on the apartment door if he saw the father's motorcycle, or if he saw him out in the yard of the funeral home playing with his daughter.

"Got a job," he'd say.

"Sure, give me a minute."

It was a quick fifteen dollars. At first it had bothered the father significantly, though he had tried not to let it. "It's just heavy lifting," he had told himself. "It happens to everyone." But it was just that, the weight of the bodies, that had bothered him.

The father went on a job with the owner of the funeral home one day to a house that was practically in the same neighborhood where they lived. The widow had died in her house and she had lived alone. There was still old coffee on the stove. She had died in her sleep, they'd said. They had found her body in bed. "No relatives," the owner of the funeral home said.

The father inquired and found that the house was for sale, and for much less than it was worth. He had a job at Levitz furniture and had managed to save money by putting it in a bean can under the kitchen counter.

When he and his wife went to look at the house, everything was the same as the day he had gone to get the body. The house had not been aired out all winter and the sunlight that came through the windows showed the particles in the air. It made the wife think of looking through the rum bottle she had dived down with to the sea floor in Bimini and filled with sea water thick with tiny shells and pieces of coral. The house was snug with antiques from the 1920s; in every drawer of the bureau, secretary and foot-peddle sewing machine were artifacts from the old couple's lives. The heavy metal razor, coat buttons, trouser socks, and some pretty snazzy hats evidenced the old man. The coffee was still on the stove. This unnerved the wife, but she liked the house and all the furniture, so she decided not to let the situation bother her. She used the old woman's spices, her laundry soap, even her rosewood shampoo. They gave away the old woman's clothes, except for her panty hose, but kept the man's, which the father wore to work, funerals, and at various other times.

Today the father returned to the house, the setting of he and his wife's marriage, for the first time since they'd separated. He had been 19 when his daughter was born. Now he had an eight year old daughter and was getting divorced. He was only 27 and had already caused so much damage. But, he was here to get his daughter and to take her out to wade in the stream next to the Sound and to play ghost baseball like he had done in the mountains of North

12

Carolina. He couldn't fathom how different he would be when she graduated from high school. He had thought about lying to her about how old he and her mother were so that she wouldn't make the same mistakes.

He stood in the city grass next to the street staring at the house. It needed painting. He had painted it brown right after they bought it. He had never cleaned the gutters. He noticed the stained, thick-slatted blinds were down. He thought about he and his daughter tossing the Nerf football back and forth, and how when it had gotten caught and gashed in the apple tree, she had put a band-aid on it.

'It's two in the afternoon,' he thought. 'Why are the blinds down, Lauren?'

He had never seemed to himself to be a sentimental person, but as he mounted the wooden stairs that he had replaced himself, he felt something like sentiment, the joy and bitter devotion to a place and time.

"Lauren," he said loudly as he knocked, trying to look around the crimson cloth that covered the other side of the tiny rectangular windows.

He heard multiple locks, then the tinny sound of the old door-knob as his daughter opened the door.

"Chris, hi, sweetheart. Where's your mother?"

"She's in bed. She's sick."

"Oh." he came in. "She didn't tell me."

The house seemed empty, as though his daughter lived there alone. He thought of the widow.

"Where are we going today, Dad?"

"I thought we'd go hiking at the park and play some base-ball. Where's your mother?" He could smell the polite smell of menthols.

"Dad, she's in bed."

"What do you mean, she's sick?"

"She's sick."

"Did she say with what?"

"No."

"How long has she been in bed?"

"Three days."

"Well, that's ridiculous. Has she been feeding you?"

"Yes. We've been eating sandwiches."

"Sandwiches. For dinner."

"Uh huh."

"Well, we'll go get you a hamburger."

He walked through the entryway to the kitchen, next to the tiny hallway that contained the doors to the bedrooms: "Lauren." He heard her cough through the closed door.

"Lauren?" He walked over and stood outside her door. He felt her listening.

"Yes?"

"Can I come in?"

"I'll talk to you when you get back."

"Okay." He leaned close to the door as though it were necessary to make her hear him; as though it made them closer. "We'll be back around 5:30."

"Get her some dinner."

"I will."

His daughter was sitting in the middle of the rough red brocade couch. He took her hand and led her through the living room as though leading her out of a store or museum.

The park was practically empty. He didn't know why, but when he had envisioned he and his daughter on their first outing alone in their broken state, he had envisioned them wading through the stream that ran along the beach of Puget Sound like they did in the summer. When they got there he realized that they probably shouldn't even play baseball. They sat in the car in the parking lot in front of the foot bridge that led over the railroad tracks.

"It's raining," he said. "I'm sorry." He felt guilty for the rain. "Do you want to go walk down to the beach for a minute? I have an umbrella in the trunk."

"Okay."

He took the black umbrella from the trunk and handed it to his daughter. She held it in front of her like she'd seen people do, but struggled to get it to stay open. He took it, latched it open for her, then handed it back.

"Dad, you'll get wet."

"That's okay, honey."

"I don't want you to get wet. You hold it."

He took it and bent down over her as they walked through the gravel that led to the metal stairs of the scaffolding-like footbridge. He had never come there without Lauren, and they had never come there without Christy.

His daughter's little shoes clunked against the steep stairs as she struggled to climb them. The stairs were slatted so that they could see through them to the ground and he wondered if she was scared. He had always carried her before. The uneven plip-plop-plip of the rain against the umbrella punctuated the sounds of their feet, creating a static-like sound in his brain.

Puget Sound appeared as they reached the platform that stood just above the trees, a salty lake-like creature, misty in the expectant calm of the aging afternoon. They stood facing East over the tracks. They knew from experience which way the train came. Looking far out to where the shoreline bent and curved to the North, they saw that no train was coming.

"You said Mom's been sick for three days?"

"I guess. She says she's sick. She's been in bed."

"Has anybody come over?"

"No, and she won't let me have anybody over either. Mary hasn't even come over. She's the only person she'll talk to on the

15

phone, besides you when you call. … Megan said Mary said Mom drinks too much."

"Does she? Have you seen her?"

"Yes, she's always carrying a glass with something she gets from the bottle in the cabinet."

"Huh." He wanted to say, 'Well, don't you worry about Mom, she's going to be fine, I'll fix this,' but he couldn't force himself.

They stood on the metal platform, not a soul to be seen. The railroad track and the shoreline divided the freshwater and sea-fed Sound from the park, bright with daisies and grass and Evergreen trees that stood still in the shapeless winter day.

All he'd ever seen Lauren drink was Bud and Rainier. He couldn't imagine her drinking like that. She must be trying to show him.

"There's no train," his daughter said.

They both thought of the day the three of them had come to see the sunset and had watched a train come around the bend, snaking toward them along the shore – it seemed to take forever to get to them – and when it had gotten close it had begun to move the ground in long shakes that felt like tall waves beneath a boat, and she had gotten a little scared, so both her parents had put a hand on each of her shoulders, then her father had picked her up and they had stood close while the train bar-reled right under them, seeming to have picked up great speed when it suddenly got close enough for them to jump down onto it, which they all thought about doing, and in the great noise that was beneath them, that would have forced them to yell if they'd wanted to talk, he remembered thinking of Christmas, of snow covering everything, the rock wall, the Subaru, the tops and sides of the bent cattails around the pond, around the tiny farmhouse in the mountains of North Carolina. He remembered standing there with the train rushing beneath them deciding to buy Lauren a winter coat, which she already needed in September, and feeling definitely that he loved her and their daughter.

"Want to go get a hamburger?" the father asked.

"Sure."

When they got back he picked up the balled-up orange wrappers from the passenger side floor and carried them to the garbage can on the side of the house. His daughter let herself in with a key. The house seemed blessedly still, like a dead wren. The leaves surrounding it had been there for months, since before he'd left. They had turned into dark brown and black compost. He felt guilty for not having come over to clean them. He didn't really want to go inside.

His daughter had left the door open for him. When he pushed it open he smelled the humid smell of boiling thyme and coriander, Lauren's corned beef boiling on the stove. The built-in shelf above the fireplace and bookshelves held Christmas cards; he recognized the ones from his family, all with the North Star, Jesus and the manger scene, and the squirrel tail he had found in the yard after Rumpus tore apart the rest of what was a particularly bloody kill, one which was apparently too torn apart to present to them on the porch. What he didn't see was the lamp with the macramé shade his wife had made hanging in the corner next to the window. It had taken her from mid-summer until Christmas, and she had given it to him with a card that said, "To study by" because he had been accepted that spring to the University of Washington.

The pictures she had torn from art books of Botticelli nudes, that his mother had called "pornography" when she and his father had visited, still graced the puce walls, brown dripping stains decorating the spaces in between from all the humidity of rainy days and boiling water.

"Where's the lamp?" he said too quietly for anyone to hear. Lauren had sat for hours in the backyard in the summer and fall on a green and white chaise lounge, pulling and twisting the thick dread-like fibers, then moved inside to the chair by the fireplace, the rough red chair that matched the couch, in the long and cozy holiday months to finish it. He had liked that

17

lampshade, the way it dotted the ceiling with mosaic shadows and lit up Christy's collection of plastic horses that stood on the tiers of the tapered corner bookshelf.

He heard Lauren in the kitchen talking to Christy. He walked through the living room and stood in the kitchen door frame.

Lauren took the lid off the pot and held it up, showing her daughter the condensation.

"Mom's teaching me how to make rain," she said.

The father saw the glass, a short unmistakable shape, of a kind he had never owned and had never seen in their house, on the kitchen table next to the stove. It looked strange on the plastic, orange-flowered table cloth.

"Where's the lamp?"

"What," Lauren said flatly, not like she didn't know what he was talking about.

"The macramé lamp."

"I threw it away."

He decided to stop there, that it was better to leave.

"I'll pick her up next Saturday."

"Sure," she said shortly.

He turned to go, then remembered his daughter, who came over and held his leg. As he walked toward the door, his daughter behind him, he felt as though he should be leaving something, a marker of some kind.

He got in the old, sturdy Rover with the rusted door and hood. It choked and shook him before it died. He pumped the gas pedal, then tried again. It cut on. He sat there, staring at the beaded up drops on the windshield. He looked up at the window where the lamp used to be.

"You can't avoid it," he thought, revving the engine to go up the hill. "It just comes after you."

The Laundromat

The street was quiet. There were many cars going home for the night from work, their lights passing, coming at them, and passing again. It was quiet; not the quiet of being covered in snow, but the humming quiet of rhythmic constancy. The street was wet with light rain and it made the sidewalks a dark gray as they walked to the grocery store not far from their house. It was something they had never done before. The red car lights were fuzzy in the misty rain and as they approached N. 85th St., the little girl could see the Chinese restaurant with its red letter lights and they were fuzzy too, in the rain.

The little girl's mother held her hand now that they were at the corner of Greenwood and N. 85th. The bank where they had an account was across the street, and they had just passed the antique shop, as well as the 1950s restaurant where her mother's best friend worked. Across Greenwood, on the corner, was another antique shop and across the street from that was a dance studio. The dance studio caused an empty feeling in the little girl, especially when it was rainy and cold because it was so large and empty. Next to the dance studio was the music store where she took clarinet lessons every Wednesday after school.

They were going to Lucky's. It was the same grocery store where they had gone ever since the little girl could remember.

They had never walked there before. The little girl, her mother and her father had usually gone there together in her father's little yellow Fiat. Occasionally, the girl and her mother had gone by themselves after school, in the dark blue Volkswagen bug, but that was mostly when the girl had taken half days at Montessori, before she'd started kindergarten. Sometimes, her father had gone by himself with a list. But never before had any combination of them walked.

The girl and her mother crossed N. 85th in the rain with their black umbrella, her mother in a brown sweater that wasn't enough for the wet September weather, and the little girl in a yellow slicker. Her mother looked very pretty with her black hair in the rain, tamped down with moisture and a little bit frizzy.

"I have to go to the grocery store," her mother had said when they were still at home. "Do you want to walk?" The little girl hadn't answered and her mother had immediately gathered the little girl's coat and the umbrella.

The girl looked up at her mother. She felt that she looked different. That she held a woeful look. The girl had never seen her mother wear her face in this way for more than a few minutes. It had been there when her mother's own mother had gotten into the bad car accident, but then the more long-lasting expression her mother's face had taken on was that of worry. The severe down-turn of mouth that her mother now wore had in the past been saved for moments of deep concern, or moments of crying, but then had dissipated. Now her mouth had the look that it had always been this way.

They passed the Chinese restaurant and then the coin and stamp shop that the girl's friend Meghan's dad had taken them to one Saturday afternoon where the little girl had bought a penny from 1857 and an envelope full of stamps from around Thailand and Botswana. She kept the penny in her nightstand, what was really an old wooden record holder, behind her books. She had decided that the coin and stamp shop was the first place she would go when she was allowed to go places by herself.

The little girl and her mother were shielded from the rain by the awnings of the businesses. Across the street was the McDonald's. When she was a baby it had been a laundromat underneath which stray cats had lived. The three of them, the little girl, her mother and father, had gone there with sheets and pillowcases full of flannel shirts, denim short shorts, and baby clothes. One night they had gone home while the laundry was drying and all of it had been stolen. Her father had been quiet all the way home, then had gone to the porch to smoke a joint and gone to bed. The next day, he had called his parents and told them what had happened. They had sent baby clothes that were nicer than the clothes from the Salvation Army that the little girl had been wearing. They had then switched laundromats.

In the summer, they hadn't gone to the laundromat. The girl's mother and Mary, her best friend, had done the wash in the backyard with the old ringer washer that had been in the basement of the house when they had bought it. But when the little girl's mother had gone to the grocery store to get tea bags to make sun tea and had witnessed, as she was driving down N. 85th Street, the old white dirty wooden building being knocked down and pulled apart, its wood walls that had been the destination of their Saturday family outings splintering like kindling, the little girl's mother was distraught. The laundromat building seemed like a large, dried-out bug, a behemoth of the antediluvian world being hauled off to disintegrate, its significance soon to exist only in her memory.

There was a large puddle under one of the awnings of a bar and the girl and her mother stepped around it and the dripping water. The mother looked down at the girl's feet to check if they were getting too wet. "We should have put on your rain boots," she said. When they got to the parking lot of Lucky's her mother stopped in front of the corral of carts in front of the store. "I don't know how we're going to get all of the groceries back. I won't be able to hold the umbrella and the groceries at the same time." She kept her hand on the cart. She wished she could talk to her daughter sort of like a girlfriend, to at least be able to explain things. She wanted to tell her how the lady who had brought them muffins was not what she seemed. She had told her daughter it was okay when she'd looked up from the gooey, undercooked mess that the woman, another mother from the preschool, had brought to the picnic in a brown basket. "She's not so into berries," she had told the woman. She felt badly now for making excuses for her daughter. She felt guilty for encouraging her to eat something not up to par. The woman was not up to par, she thought. Men don't care, she wanted to tell her daughter. Sometimes, they just don't care.

Her daughter stood next to her, next to the grocery cart. The rain splashed against the metal of the cart, sometimes the big drops splashing onto their bare hands. The little girl thought about her dad. She thought how if he were there, there would be no questioning. They would go inside. They would get food. He would get her one of the donuts from the bakery counter to eat while they were shopping. She would sit under the cart and let him push her, though lately she had preferred to walk beside him while her mother put things into the cart.

"I think maybe we should go to McDonald's," her mother said. Her mother never took her to McDonald's. The only time she ever got to eat at McDonald's was when her friend's parents took her. She often thought about the day when she could go to the stamp and coin shop and then afterward to McDonald's by herself.

"Maybe go in and just get some things for breakfast first," her mother said.

They went inside the grocery store and walked over to the cereal and breakfast aisle. There were a lot of breakfast foods that the little girl and her dad liked. He liked to get Grape Nuts and pancake mix and Mrs. Butterworth's syrup, while the little girl got Quaker Maple & Brown Sugar oatmeal and Carnation Breakfast Bars. The little girl's favorite part of going to the grocery store was standing with her father in front of the

Carnation Breakfast Bars and talking about what kinds to get. He would ask her what flavors she was in the mood for and talk about how many combinations they had or tell her what sounded good to him. She had asked him why he didn't eat them and he had said they were too sweet. She made the point that he ate pancakes with syrup on them, but he said that was a special thing he reserved for himself for the weekends, which is when he went jogging, too, but if he ate Carnation Breakfast Bars he would probably eat them too often and then he would get fat. This had made her laugh. She couldn't imagine her father fat. He was thinner than any other dad she knew.

The little girl's mother didn't often eat breakfast. She put some oatmeal and Cream of Wheat, which she ate sometimes on the weekends on really cold days, into the cart.

The little girl stood in front of the Carnation Breakfast Bars. They were daunting. The last time she had gotten Peanut Butter Crunch. Her father never let her get the same flavor more than twice in a row. He said it wasn't good to be too much a creature of habit, only old people were allowed to eat the same things all the time. She already got the same thing every time at Guadalajara, the Mexican restaurant they went to. She couldn't see anything except Peanut Butter Crunch. She forced herself to read and process the meaning of another label. S' mores. Didn't sound good at all. She couldn't reach the Peanut Butter Crunch, it was on the top shelf.

She looked over at her mother. She was staring at the Grape Nuts.

"Mom. Can you get this down for me?"

It was still raining and the parking lot had a black oil-slickness as they shuffled out of the store with their one paper bag under the mother's arm.

They crossed the parking lot and went to the corner. The red "Don't Walk" light was flashing, so they waited, the little girl half under the umbrella, the hair that was sticking out from her hood getting wet. They both watched the traffic going by, small hydroplanes of water under the car tires making the sound of rushing water. Her mother looked over at the McDonald's. She thought how that one thing had changed the neighborhood, legitimizing and destroying it in some way, making it modern by taking away its origins.

The mother wondered if her daughter knew; if she knew that her mother was waiting. During the week, the little girl was used to her father getting home after she went to bed, and only seeing him sleeping through a crack in the door in the mornings when she got her tiny, heavy coat out of the hall closet. The little girl always looked in on her father through the crack. Recently, her mother had told her he was out of town. But the next weekend he was coming, and they would have to talk about it.

The mother tried to think about what it would be like to do things with her daughter on her own. They could make frozen chocolate bananas and leave them in the freezer until they'd eaten them all at their leisure, for a month if they liked. "He'll come over and look in the freezer," she thought. "He'll come over and look in the freezer to see if I'm doing okay, to see if I'm keeping the right things in there."

She thought about how it would have been just like any other relationship if they hadn't gotten married. The furniture they bought would still have come from the furniture store where he worked part-time to put himself through school and from Salvation Army. The pots and pans, the alfalfa sprout growing kit, the macramé lamps her best friend had made for them, the Botticellis torn from art books, the air heavy with greasy condensation that stuck to and dripped down the walls, all the same as it would have been if they hadn't married each other. But that they had gotten married made it sadder to her in some way. Their things had a life story that would change; where they had bought them, and when, just like if they had been bought in another relationship, but their being married and then one day not would draw a very stark line. Even if one or the other of them had bought them, they had bought them for each other, for their marriage. Everything was for their marriage. Everything was for each other.

26

The story couldn't continue as though she had brought the tiny dresser or pair of wool pants from Salvation Army or the book, even, home one day for herself alone.

She had planted the sprouts one Sunday morning while he was asleep. The sun had shone on the foam green tiles flecked with yellow and red of the kitchen floor, and she had looked through the window filled in its frame with the bright yellow glow of forsythia blossoms, out at the apple and cherry trees of their yard, and had allowed herself to be engulfed by the daunting contented sleepwalk of married life. Her husband in the bedroom sleeping-in, her daughter, a baby then, sleeping, too, but about to wake, needing nothing but this womb of blown glass that was their home.

The mother didn't know if she and, consequently, the situation was the way that it was because the one thing her parents had said they'd agreed upon about raising her was that she be independent. She worried that their ideas about this had been so different that it had made her too independent, more independent than they'd ever wanted. She worried that it had just been an excuse for them not to have had to come to an agreement about how to raise their daughter, to decide what the right direction was. She felt that no guidance was misguidance. She felt that she had no direction.

She took her daughter's hand as they stepped off the curb to cross the eveningstreet, the cars on either side of the crosswalk seeming like horses at the banks of a river. They turned left onto Greenwood Avenue N., passing another bank, a sub shop, the only shoe repair store she knew of anymore, a soul food restaurant, an Italian restaurant, a doughnut shop. Next to the doughnut shop was the McDonald's. It was brightly lit with people seated at the plastic booths eating fries and hamburgers, drinking sodas and milkshakes. She opened the door for her daughter. Her daughter looked up at her, but didn't say anything as she walked through the door.

The mother remembered that she liked McDonald's. She liked

27

their little yellow papered cheeseburgers. She used to take her daughter and her friends there after preschool. She had stopped going because her husband had made her feel guilty about "feeding that shit to our daughter."

The large number of people eating quickly, with such clear purpose, made her grateful. The fluorescent lights, the beeping of the fryers being done, the sharp, "Anything else?"s had the familiarity of safety in numbers.

She stood in line with great gratitude, as though it were Christmas and she'd had nowhere to go. She looked down at her daughter, who was not looking up at the menu, but looking around at the big bodies flanking her like trees in a forest.

"Mom, I want a cheeseburger and Chicken McNuggets. If I don't finish the McNuggets, I can save them for later."

"Okay, sweetie. Do you want to share my fries? How about a milkshake or a Coke?"

"I'll have a chocolate shake, and I'll share your fries." She smiled up at her mother, and her mother realized that she hadn't seen her look that happy since dinner the past Sunday when her father had pretended to be the wind at the park, blowing her face and her hair while she closed her eyes and laughed. He had left that night after their daughter had gone to sleep.

They stood next to the counter waiting for their food. The mother thought of how the spot she was standing on used to be surrounded by round circle-faced machines kaleidoscopically turning their clothes around. The father used to stand outside smoking and looking at the people walking by, or would sit in one of the plastic chairs doing physics equations. The mother would stand in the alley of washers, watching their daughter wander around looking into the portholes at the clothes flipping and flopping around, looking deeply into the detergent machine slots and their contents, or standing in the doorway "with" her father while he smoked. Sometimes, they would dance; a sort of a waltz, slow and led by the father, who felt his daughter's little hands leaning into his, waiting to be shown by feel what to do next. The evening air had come in through the open front door, replacing some of the heat in the steamy box that the laundromat had become as their clothes tumbled through their cycles. There had not often been other people in the laundromat.

The mother looked around at all the people eating through the din of fast food. Now that he was gone these people were comforting. It was a kinship of many kinds of desperation; at the very least they had not had enough time or endurance to make dinner for themselves or their families and had given in, relenting in the face of difficulty, taking comfort in meat, oil, and sugar.

There they stood: where once had been a stone floor was now a stone floor painted white with cheap paint. Where once had been wood walls were now brightly clean windows with fluorescent lights' reflections. Where once were rows of machines designed to help better their lives were bright red and yellow images rising up like monuments. And, most heartbreaking, where once had been a dominion of cats beneath the wooden framework was now a wasteland, its edges dripping with water when it rained, no longer a shelter.

The mother watched the fryers. For some reason her stare, the nervous stare of waiting, was always taken back to the fryers. When they dumped the new batch of finished fries into the metal holding container, hot from the oil, she pulled her daughter close to her side, hugging her tight.

Vienna Sausages

Marie looked upward through the defrost-capable glass of the Lima bean to the back heads of Lila and Tommy, the transistor cigarette lighter TV between them. Telephone poles were staked like fire lookouts on the horizon. Marie lay in the backseat surrounded by her stuffed friends. All afternoon they had been skirting the fur trader hills and chapel window rivers of Montana. Sometimes she and Tommy would play hangman. Lila looked out the window, too. She liked to watch for the Motel 6s and Super 8s; they looked like space stations, lit up, waiting for them to pull up and attach for refueling.

The beds had pinball machine appendages. Before Marie got under the plant bed of rayon and polyester she popped a quarter in and was jarred around like a bean sorter. In the morning the housekeepers would kindly smile as they invaded their fox burrow. The rotary phone would start ringing its recess bell ring, the front desk calling, clamoring in an effort to send them back into the world of pavement and dust.

It was warm and Lila had the window rolled down. Her black hair blew in and out of the window like a swarm of crows. Marie lay in back, content with routine. She was missing third grade. Lila had been so tall and comprehensible going to Marie's school to ask. The teacher had told her, really nonchalantly, that yeah,

31

they'd be doing some things, some exercises, problems, but nothing Marie hadn't shown she could do with enthusiasm and speed, and as she had been called Brainiac by the other kids, and took unbelievable sportsman's enthusiasm at find-the-book-in-the-stacks at the school library, even having made the library into a lunchtime clubhouse for she and her friends, other nonbookenthusiast kids harassing them, Mrs. Chee thought it would be fine for Marie to go to a tropical island for the next year.

Marie watched the oncoming scenery through the too steeply slanted back window of the hatchback, filled past safety's brim with books and T-shirts and fishing poles and things she knew not of because she didn't know what they kept in their drawers and closets. She lay in the seat mold created by the comforter and pillows and her brightly colored cohorts, watching the phone and electrical lines tick by, the clouds floating like pinecones on the water.

"Honey, we'll be stopping in a minute. Think about what snacks you want to tide you over until dinner. They might have Vienna Sausages. You had them when you were about three or four, when we went with your dad fishing at the Kettle River."

Marie remembered camping, Eddy filled with rustic, enthusiastic outdoor quality, fresh air and mountain vigor. He'd had long hair and cut-off jeans shorts. They all had.

The light changed when they pulled into Union 76. It was instantly cooler in the shade of the convenience store mud hut. The attendants milled around like pill bugs between the Fred Flintstone house and the cars docked at the filling stations. The ramshackle head had all manner of scum on the walls and a cheap linoleum floor that was being incorporated back into the earth. When Marie came out she didn't see Lila or Tommy. She walked along the cement fringe boardwalk of the convenience store scanning for them, and finally caught sight of them off to the side of the parking lot talking by the car. Lila wasn't really talking, more like refereeing between Tommy and himself, her stance cool and easygoing, his like the true and loyal right hand of a king, having to call upon intuition ceaselessly, trying to help and thereby touch the untouchable. Marie was instinctually worried about Lila, but was drawn to the dense salty goodness of the brine-candied sausages, and anything Lila was genuinely excited about, so she left them to their mysterious sideshow.

Marie and Lila had a pact. It was unspoken but certain. Small as she was, Marie knew that she was Lila's favorite person in the world. Senseless as it was, Marie was the only person she would have been able to talk to had she become unable to speak, had she gone crazy, had her language, her mind left her. Lila was often specific. She liked to refer to things with specificity; Calumet Baking Powder, ask a person to hand her that masking tape with "I love you, Mom" written in pencil on it, the blue bowl that looked like it had beaded jewels on the rim, the dish towel Mary had given her eight Christmases ago; the coat Edward hadn't let her buy. This specificity made her genuine, even when you didn't think she was.

Tommy was a garter snake or something as innocuous. He was harmless, but it was hard to understand him. He could be fun, silly fun, historical knowledge fun, and it was hard not to respect him for his ability to adapt, to wind his way through the tall grass. But there was nothing obviously useful about him for his own sake. Maybe he ate bugs; he had to serve some function in the ecosystem. But he was not built for the tasks he was given in his daily life. Marie wondered, when he told her stories of going to Scandinavia in his youth, what magic he could have created if he'd been allowed to run free, before he was caught by a barn owl.

They had met at the university, where Lila had returned after she kicked Eddy out. Marie had stood that day at the big picture window that was strangely opulent in their little brown house, watching Lila kick the tires on the blue Volkswagen bug as Eddy drove away from the square of cement that said, "Edward loves Lila," with her name underneath, all of them inside a big star, as though they were stranded in a supernova together, their names carved in for eternity witha large stick, that moment of acknowledged love in 1976 undeniable, the beauty of their characters etched into the future like leadless pencil tracings. It was all clear and permanent there in the street.

The extreme air conditioning ambushed Marie and made her feel brave and far from home. She walked over to the cooler with its maddening array of colors and packaging, and picked out an orange juice in a box, like milk. She started down one aisle, eying Nutter Butters, thinking it was strange how they sounded good but were not something she'd ever sought out, only had at a friend's birthday or house or house or something, noting that this was the aisle with cookies, she loved cookies, and knew she must be nearing the Hostess stand, Ding Dongs, Suzy Qs and Donettes, and she thought of the candy she got depending on her mood, depending on the season, at the 7-11 on the corner back in Seattle, blow pops and Bubble Yum and ice cream sandwiches, candy a necessary part of winding down after school, something she simply did.

She found the place where they shelved the canned meat; she had never thought of SPAM, tuna fish, and the prized Vienna Sausages as being in the same category before, but there they all were, all in the war rations section.

Lila walked up next to Marie lightly, like a scarf blowing in the wind.

"Oh good, they have them," Lila reached in front of her, "Take five or so," she grabbed them off the shelf in an irrational clamor, "They'll be good to have for later."

She left Marie standing in the aisle and walked over the empty checkout terminal, guarded by magazine stands and flanked on all sides by jerky and cigarettes. Tommy came in and went over to the cooler. Marie followed Lila out the door.

The rest of the day Lila smoked and told Tommy what it had been like stealing chairs with Edward, and running down the corridor to escape and conceive, until they'd found themselves in Key West. Marie slept. When she woke in the late afternoon, she looked around the car not knowing she was satisfied, but not feeling anxious because she wasn't doing anything after being so studious, after composing and skateboarding; not having a moment without duty in all her seven years. She looked around, thought of the hills out there like a rustic dream, what it would be like to be scuffing up their dust, walking in between them, to have no distractions but the job of feeding yourself, but then nothing would come from a can and she would have to pick things, to either kill or have the desire to eat things that had just been killed, and not be able to forget that you had to kill to eat them; the night would feel so lonely with the ghosts around the campfire, wondering then, appreciating what it was like to have a conscience again, to be born into the killing and the blanket of instinct and the comfort of the dead stars coming to them like needle pricks in her mother's thick, dark curtains, spraying their light across the early green earth.

She came out of her sleep haze with these thoughts and felt the pleasantness of being hungry. Her mother was staring out the window to the dark closing in around her, memories of sitting in the old Chevy smoking cigarettes. Her 16 year old mind tortured by her mother's determination to replace her own beautiful simplicity with someone else's decadent, static dream. Marie sat up as fully as she could with the supplies on the floor behind their seats, and heard the rustle of a plastic bag under her right foot. She remembered what was in it. The can was compact and sweet looking with its wrap-around label pictoral of the little wieners in blue and brown, festive as a Southern pig pickin'. She had never popped the lid on a can before, but wedged her thumb under the little ring until she realized this was not the best way and switched fingers. The can popping startled Lila, who turned around and smiled. "Want one?" Marie said.

"No, that's okay. … Well, maybe. Sure. They started making those when I was a teenager and I'd eat them when I'd go camping by myself along the James River. Those and molasses beans. The water looked muddy but when I dipped my cup in it to drink it it was as clear as tap water."

The sausages sat snugly in their compact ring like a carburetor.

35

The tinny meat smell dispersed into the car and filled them both with satisfaction. Their existence was seemingly nonessential in that vast land, like the motels, but the reality of their existence nonetheless was the only thing keeping them from falling into the earth.

She pulled them out individually, like fingers, each an echo of evenings at home, doing calligraphy by the fire, playing with the dripping wax, molding it into shapes, making sausage-shaped replicas of her own fingers by pouring wax onto them, pressing it against her skin like the thin, soft paper of her Grandmother's hand resting on her own in church.

She bit them off, each with the dusky smell of old underwear and the texture of her lips when she covered them in Vaseline. She ate them as they drove past the rolled up boles of hay like corn on the cob sitting in the fields, threshing machines about to be done for the day, horses and cows flicking their tales in the twilight. The misplaced things between them solidifying and scurrying off into the wild where the desert rodents ran out of the corners of their eyes.

Dusk on the road; permanence and a tranquil settling down of mood and heat. They were as air-packed inside the lime green Saab, the wind blowing in shifts, stirring outside, inside cool and warm, the Nightly News a black and white shrill of movement, it and the movements on the forefront of the horizon a mockery of their stillness. Marie and Lila liked to watch the sky settle down, the scene change between blue cloudiness and stars, the extremeness upsetting if they thought about it, the sun going to the other side of the earth, the earth twisting and turning like a rusted metal top.

"Honey, we'll be stopping soon. We're near Whitefish, where I fished the last time I was in Montana, before you were born. We'll get a river cabin and go fishing in the morning before we get on the road. If you catch anything we can pack it in the cooler and cook it at the next motel, probably near Elk, tomorrow night."

She and Tommy had been passing a beer back and forth for about two hours. It wasn't the same beer of course. The boxes accumulated in the kitchen next to the back door, then on the back porch, Marie never saw them clear them out, though they must have sometimes. She had no knowledge of alcohol's effects, no judgment. She didn't know it was trashy to keep stacks of beer boxes or to give your child the bottle caps off of Lucky's that had the puzzles on them. She thought the puzzles were fun – "I see your soapbox racer."

Marie was always wide awake at night. Her bedtime had been set for around ten, though she had watched David Letterman enough to dispute this. The time before they pulled into a motel for the night was pleasant, like coming to the end of a race she knew she was going to win. The warm sense of deserving a comfortable bed and pleasant, meaningful dreams.

The lights flashing behind them were jarring, as though someone had come upon them in an alley to grab their backpacks and walkman. Lila took the beer from Tommy into her lap and sat up straight, drinking it directly in front of her. Tommy eased on to the side of the road, into the soft, rocky earth. The wind no longer streamed around the car and Marie could hear the crickets singing loudly and could feel the secrecy for the first time, what she had recognized as self-assurance in Lila when she had come to her school suddenly became a red curtain, and behind it a whole theater full of curtains.

Lila opened her door and began to pour out the beer as the officer came over to Tommy's window. Marie watched fixed as Lila poured out the beer with one hand, the other on her bare leg just below her cutoff jean shorts, while the officer asked Tommy where he was going and why he had been going so fast. It seemed fantastically privileged what she was seeing, the turning of a card to the other side of her mother's personality, like someone who's just come off a stage.

There was more tension in Tommy's voice than usual, more than there was when he tried to calm Lila down at night when she was worried about her mother sitting in the nursing home washed in the undertow of her past, or when he was complimenting her on her tacos or fried chicken, trying not to overdo it. But the calm of Lila's ring-filled fingers pouring out the beer at the side of the road, the sureness of her steady hand on her leg, made Marie know it would be fine. Among the blue red and white lights flashing against the country darkness, Marie looked down into her lap at the sausages she held that her mother had gotten for her, watched as Lila tucked the empty beer can into the opening between her seat and the door frame. Marie held to the thought of eating her nighttime snack as soon as the officer, the traveling salesman stuck at their threshold, was gone, mimicking her mother's hunted silence.

The Mirage of Mario Sanchez

When he opened his eyes to the stagnant but tidy room – its high wood walls and floors, the furniture that said, "I know you," but not too much, and the faint light that outside was the hot sun – it told him only that he was there. He had read "The Lost Decade" at the bidding of his wife, but he didn't see the tragedy in it. His wife, Cella, made wood furniture, carving it out in symbiotic patterns that to her went on forever, past the back of the chair and the edge of the cabinet door. He thought her work was nice, and she like an orphan girl radiating through her rags while following the lathe like the back of a centipede, yet he chastised her passion for it and didn't understand the spiritual and philosophical value she saw there. When she'd asked him to leave he'd thought of it simply as an incentive to get out of the house.

Each morning he puts his right forefinger in his mouth, takes it out for a moment, then tastes it. This isn't to check the movement of the air. He feels he has become quite perceptive in his exile, and when he tastes the air he feels as though he's able to taste the distillation of the entire day to come. Today it tastes a little off. Not tragically so, just a little odd -– like maybe a mighty, flabby woman will streak past him, or maybe he'll see a toddler trotting along licking a huge pinwheel lollipop the size of its face and suddenly it will trip and fall face down upon it, like a sticky shield that will attract ants immediately. Or some tourist who's had a good day fishing will decide to buy the entire crowd at the Turtle a couple of rounds, which had happened before. It changed the atmosphere of the bar to that of a carnival for an hour or so.

When he'd been with Cella he'd almost always drunk alone, but now every day he came effervescently to the Turtle, called there by what seemed like an obligation to his new identity. There were four bartenders at the Turtle, and he was friendly with them all, but of the four Bob on weekdays and Cat on weekends were his favorites. For the most part he also had more congenial memories of them. Bob let Stephen drink well past his obvious limit on many occasions, which Stephen appreciated. He wasn't exactly a gentleman, but he was a soft drunk; he'd fall off his stool before he'd ever be lewd or obnoxiously belligerent.

It was Wednesday. He'd always hated Wednesdays because he felt that Wednesday was the least dramatic day of the week, save for Tuesday, but he was born on a Tuesday. Wednesdays made him lonely. On Wednesdays he sometimes thought of Cella's flowery air and how she'd always have the windows open and never seemed to be cold. Sometimes on Wednesdays he thought of changing his routine, maybe just taking a walk, but he never had. And lately the Wednesday gloom had been worse; he was running out of money.

"Come on lad," Bob the bartender said in a very fake Irish accent, "Tell me what's got you saggin' or I'll haveta heave-ho ya outa here."

"Nothing."

"But you're sippin' insteada sluggin', lad ..." he patted Stephen's cheeks. "You look sick, sister. Come on, level with me ..."

"Alright, fine." Stephen leaned over the bar, "I'll let you in on the secret, but when I stop comin' in next week some time you gotta cover for me ... say you heard I went snorkeling in the Bahamas."

42

Bob had his ear cocked right over Stephen's Seven-and-Seven with his eyebrows up.

"I'm broke."

Bob jumped back and slapped the counter, "Get outa here!"

"Down to my last two thousand."

"Now that ain't exactly broke ..."

"It's broke to me," he sipped his drink. "Especially here."

"You got that part right anyway ... mmm mmm mmm ... Mmm! Whatchou gonna do?"

"Don't know ... I may have to call my wife."

"I hear ya, I guess when you retire too early you ain't got no feed when the cows come home," he started wiping the counter and wiped over to another customer, shaking his head as he led himself across the boxing-ring bar. "Mmm mmm mmm."

'Why'd I tell him that?' Stephen asked himself. He felt violated. He hadn't analyzed too many things about himself consciously, but, faced with the potential of poverty, he realized that he felt as though an edge were dulling. He put a five on top of the twenty that already sat on the bar next to his drink and soaked napkin and stood up. It was early afternoon. Bob was resting on one hip talking to his customer with his back to Stephen and didn't notice him walk out of the open-air bar.

Stephen had had four drinks but was still very sober. The sidewalks of the small island were half taken over by elephant-ear sized leaves and as he attempted to stroll he felt self-conscious veering around them, as though people might think he were stumbling. The sidewalk seemed unpaved, uprooted as it had been by Banyan tree roots, uneven, rural-seeming and coarse. What was he going to do without money? The rent for the small furnished apartment with the polished wood floors was a thousand a month. It was the 27th. He didn't know how long he could last on a thousand dollars – he'd never added up his expenses. Regardless, he'd soon be out of a place to live. He was sweating through his white ramie shirt and envisioned himself suddenly eclipsed by the sun, going mad in a dark alley like Jack the Ripper. 'I was almost a lawyer ...' he thought. But the thought of working felt like the word entrapment. Entrapment. 'Not only trapped, but framed, like a defenseless moron. Framed.' He stumbled through the streets, though to passersby he was only walking; a well-dressed man on his way to meet someone or out on an errand. An ordinarily brilliant soul rotting in the embalmed body of a rich man, flawless.

He had walked about three blocks when he turned down an alley-street which had music diffusing into the humid air from someone's back yard. Stephen realized he had a cigarette in his mouth, though he didn't know how long it had been there. He had felt hurried, but deliberately slowed to look through the gaping red hibiscus that seemed to grow wild there to a little white house that was as bright as a bleached white sheet; his wife always used white sheets and shook them out in the breeze of her open windows. There was a clearness around the little house. It had a little wooden blue jay next to the house number. As he passed it he noticed an old gentleman at the side of the house, partially on the lawn, partially on the unpaved drive, which was bordered by an old wooden fence, standing in front of a wooden table.

"Lo there," he waved to Stephen. Stephen stopped and took the cigarette out of his mouth.

"You lost?" he smiled and looked up from what he was doing.

"No, no," Stephen cleared his throat and lit the cigarette. "Just out for a stroll." He felt his face – he shaved every morning and it was smooth.

"You live aroun' here?" the man had an accent Stephen didn't know. He was pointing bits of color and white onto a board with a small brush.

"Yes, sir."

"You an' your wife?"

"Yes."

"Where's your wife on theese fine day?"

"She's at home – doesn't like the heat."

"Wrong place for her then," he laughed.

"That's what I tell her." He looked past the old man to where things began to get blurry.

"You wan' to come an' see?" he pointed to the piece of wood on the table.

Stephen walked among the rough white rocks until he was a few feet from the old man. Their chalk stuck to his black dress shoes. He peered over the space as though the old man were behind a partition, roped off.

"Come closer."

Stephen could see what the old man was painting with his fingers and a brush whose bristles were splayed out like an old toothbrush, like the one he'd had as a kid.

"Ice cream," said the old man. "Not like to-day – real ice cream … glace." There was a man with a cart vending ice cream by white and red bathing cabins on the beach. All the colors were bright and proud, natives. "That man was an entrepreneur," the old man said, "He know where to sell hees ice cream."

"It's wonderful," said Stephen.

"I give eet to you when I finish – tomorrow."

"Oh no …"

"Don' worry, I give to you. I no charge a poor man."

Stephen looked at him. He held his dying cigarette at his side. He looked down at the table and saw everything on it like a pinwheel spinning; brushes, bright circles of paint, tubes, a cloth, the wood with dried and drying paint all over it. "I'll come back tomorrow," he said.

"Good," said the old man. Stephen nodded once. "See you tomorrow," the old man said as Stephen turned and walked as lightly as he could down the rough drive to the sidewalk.

He felt like having a soda, a pop, like when he was a kid. It seemed he hadn't had plain soda since then. There was a store on the corner across the street from his apartment. As he turned onto the sidewalk he glanced back toward the old man who was not there any longer. He looked around and down the alley-street. There were some old men three houses down playing cards at a square table at the edge of a flat driveway. There was an old woman two houses down from them and across rocking on her front porch. There were two chickens criss-crossing each other in a hurry, and the sounds of them and children from a block over. There was the music coming into and out of the air like breath. He looked back up the old man's drive – no old man, no table, no glace. Stephen turned around and went back the way he had come.

Once he was back at the apartment he sat on the bed. 'Man,' he looked around at the contrived living space. 'I'm going to turn into a freakin' nutball.' He lay back and watched the ceiling fan until he fell asleep.

He was hot and crumpled and uncomfortable, wanting incredibly much to let go of his mother's hand, though he knew he couldn't. His mother was beautiful, as all mothers are to their sons.

"Mama, can I please have some glace?"

She looked down at him and out at the sea. He was aware of strings from his brown cut-off trousers tickling his knees. He was barefoot.

"Do you have a nickel, son?"

"No."

As they passed the ice cream cart Stephen noticed it was the old man vending – he being himself as a boy and also outside himself, watching. He looked longingly at the white-handled wooden cart, knowing the sweet smoothness of the mango glace that was inside. The old man took out a shallow paper cone and filled it half with mango and half with mammie ice cream, and handed it to Stephen.

"I'm sorry, sir, not to-day," said Stephen's mother, her red-brown hair blowing almost away from her in the sea breeze.

"Don' worry, ma'am," the old man said, "You get me back an-o-ther day." He bent down to Stephen and whispered as he handed him the glace, "I no charge a poor man."

Stephen sat up straight in bed with his slicked black hair stuck to his forehead and face. The room was so quiet; he had never known it to be so. The noise of cars, mopeds and people talking, even yelling, seemed to be in a bottle tossed away from the captive and self-contained silence of his room. He sat up in bed, the lining of his light blue pants making a slick sound against his bare legs. His childhood room had been light blue, "sky blue," and his mother had painted white clouds across it. Cirrus and cumulus, he remembered. He put his hands over his face and brought them down slowly, sliding with the thick sweat. He couldn't even feel the ceiling fan it was moving so slowly.

'I know I have a pencil,' he thought, 'If I could only draw something …' He went over to the table by the window, but there was just a pocketknife on the dark varnished wood. In the kitchen, set off barely from the living room at a depth of four lonely feet, he found a golf pencil in the silverware drawer. It was from Oregon. He smelled it. He sat on the bed with the yellow and white striped sheet that had been furnished him, with his stubby golf pencil and an American Express bill envelope and commenced to draw a portrait of Cella. 'Just a line,' he thought as he tried to define the details of her face in his mind, the real shape of it. 'Just a line to begin – a line is all you need.' He placed the pencil to the envelope and his hand drew a quick, curvaceous line for him; he hadn't realized he was shaking. He quickly retracted his hand from the paper and closed his eyes. 'I'm a bastard … a real bastard.' He looked around the room; wood table, chairs and nightstand, wood doors, wood-framed clock, driftwood hanging on the audacious stucco wall, wood everything, it seemed; the windows even had wooden shutters. 'It's all drawn,' his thoughts stuttered as he imagined someone, people, making all that his room alone contained. 'Everything.'

He sat still until the dark came and the now strangling complexities of his little room softened; he was a stranger to his room at that hour, yet he felt welcome, as though it had been waiting for him. Soon he would start the throwing up, the convulsive terror of withdrawal, but as the liquid sense of a warm night settled over him he wanted only to sit in peace; a few moments more as captain at the end of his pirated plank.

Wax

The smell of chicken in a pan complimented the sound and smell of the fire. Her father was on the couch watching "Wild Kingdom." Lucille had stopped playing the flute in order to listen to her mother in the kitchen, to try and feel what she was doing. She watched a white candle on the light wood dining table flicker a little. It gave to her the illusion of being clear, but she could not see through it. The dining table was shiny, it had come polished when her father bought it from the furniture store where he worked, on sale. Sometimes she worked its surface with a freeze of furniture polish, liking the sound the can made and the feeling of having an unofficial duty to honor her father.

The room was quiet; despite the sound of grease in the kitchen, her mother opening jars and drawers and cabinets, she could hear the low pop of the fire, and the comforting sound of the narrator.

She looked at the cabinet built into the mantle. It was clear glass. Puppets she'd made in fifth grade, pumpkin man and Dracula, sat in front of Anna Karenina and A Tale of Two Cities on the bottom shelf. On the middle shelf were letters that were special to her mother, and Dubliners, A Portrait of the Artist as a Young Man, and Chamber Music, as well as an unframed picture of a painting of a woman standing underneath a tree, holding her child. Lucille had taken one of her mother's books from the shelf one night and read it by the fire. It had felt very strange to take something out of the cabinet. The cabinet gave off the feel of a museum, and her mother had placed the things inside while Lucille had been at school.

She dipped her finger into the pool of wax inside the red candle. It hurt a little, but red didn't hurt as much as white, she remembered. She wondered why they only sat at this table at Thanksgiving. When she was very little, her father used to sit at this table stacking pancakes onto his plate and covering them with syrup, periodically giving pieces to Scuzzy the cat. Now he ate on the couch. Her mother almost always said she'd eat later, and would eat alone in the kitchen while her father was shaving, or after he'd gone to bed. As Lucille lay in bed at night, she felt as though she were spying on her mother.

The wax caps sat on each of her fingers like printers' thumbs; she thought they looked like galoshes. She wanted to show her father, but he was so quiet when he was watching TV before dinner. Really she wanted to ask him to play Scrabble.

She took the wax off her fingertips and melted it together into a ball, which she shaped into a horseshoe. It was for her father, but she didn't know if she would give it to him. She made another ball of wax into a plump heart for her mother.

When they'd lived in New Hampshire, she'd gone sledding with her father often, while her mother stayed inside making bread or sweet potatoes or borscht. "Come on out," her father had yelled, motioning with his hand, when he saw her mother at the window. Her mother would smile at them, then disappear as though she'd been a cloud of steam. She wondered why her mother hadn't let herself enjoy the crisp, pure day when everything is frozen down tight and you walk upon the thin crust of snow as though on a pond.

"Dinner's ready," her mother said, carrying two plates of fried chicken, mashed potatoes and beans. Lucille watched her father as he muted the TV and looked over at her. She thought his eyes looked moist, as though he were about to cry, but he took the plate and smiled up at her mother. "Thank you so much," he said.

"You're welcome. You eating at the table?" she said to Lucille.

"Yes," she said. "I like being near the fire."

"You could sit on the red chair," her mother said, referring to the rough red patterned chair Lucille had once fallen asleep in that sat on the other side of the fireplace. The next morning her mother had awoken her with a pile of kittens, singing "Rise and shine, baby, Rise and shine, the sun is shining and the day is thine!"

"No, that's okay," she said.

"You going to eat with us?" her father said.

"No, I'm not hungry now."

"Well, I'm sure it's delicious," he said. "You'll enjoy it."

Her mother set the plate in front of Lucille. She smelled like wildflowers. It was a sachet she had made from flowers on the hillside overlooking the drive-in of her hometown. She had come to know the smell as symbolizing memory. The scent was her Great-Grandmother's house on the hillside, her biscuits, the habit of eating in the kitchen. The lilt of her Great-Grandfather playing old mountain songs in the living room, recalling the ways of before he was born.

Her father was still watching "Wheel of Fortune." Vanna White had always fascinated both of them. They had talked about it.

"I like Vanna," she'd said to her father one night.

"She's so consistent, but warm," her father had said.

She agreed with him. She didn't often disagree with her father. He was an agreeable man, she guessed, compared to a lot of people. She wasn't so sure about her mother.

When she'd finished eating, she looked into the cabinet again. A Tale of Two Cities' cover was wildly colorful; it reminded her in an obscure way of a caravan. Once, years before, her father had told her about the desert of Arabia, how it stretched far enough for nomads to spend their entire lives walking through it and not even cross it. They would weave with thread they'd traded spices for; spices that they'd gathered and dried by the fire. They used bright colors, reds, oranges, yellows, like the cover of A Tale of Two Cities. She had asked her father why nomads wandered the desert, and he had said that nomads wandered the desert, climbed mountains, passed through every type of terrain; there were even some in downtown Kansas City.

Did you ever want to be a nomad? She'd asked.

No.

How long do nomads stay in one place?

Not long, usually.

How long?

Long enough to learn what they need to know.

Do they have children?

Sometimes.

I don't want to be a nomad, she'd said.

That's good, her father had said.

Looking over at her father she wondered if he wasn't a nomad, but then she thought he wasn't. Probably in his mind, she thought.

When she finished, she took her plate in to her mother. Her mother was sitting at her little writing table by the stove with a book open which she wasn't looking at. Lucille walked over and put the plate in the big rectangular sink. She felt her mother listening. Her father was listening, too. She saw snow falling outside the window above the sink. She watched some of the flakes blow forth in sudden, hard gusts against the window, while most floated down toward the ground, landing gently, one upon the other.

Wish You Were Here

When I first arrived there was no color. The city looked wet as in a painting and there was a fog but it was not cold. I hadn't been prepared for the feeling of importance around me, or of the idiotic conspicuousness of my big blue backpack. There was the calm of one thing passing and another taking its place without consequence. It seemed the French understood each other. There were the opportunists; hookers and chestnut vendors, the long-armed poets of the café, salon keepers and food dealers opened out into the lush gray air; the students of the Sorbonne with their stung expressions, the heir presumptives and the heir apparents, and there was the river. I didn't talk to anyone for three days except the daytime hotel clerk. To him I'd said good morning because he'd given me a slight smile that seemed genuine. For breakfast I had an apple pastry and coffee and cream from a small grocery that reminded me of the ones in San Francisco, and walked along the quay where they still sold live chickens, and after three days felt very much a part of something important as I had never felt before.

On the third evening Brian arrived at the hotel and on the fourth day the others came. There were twenty of us in the program and we were lucky to have ten men and ten women, they said. It seemed it should have been boys and girls even though we were in college. I met Brian in the baggage room where he was stuffing his beanbag chair of a duffel bag into one of the wire-encased bins while I checked my backpack for a good razor. He had the flushed cheeks of a pure-bred and was the nervous type whose nervousness comes from feeling like he should always be doing something for you. We had coffee and took a short walk together down the streets that were the color of burlap the night I met him, and I found myself much more able to look around when I wasn't alone. He bought me a warm bag of chestnuts which I romanticized very deeply.

We went South to Avignon after five days in Paris. My new school mates played cards on the train; at least one in four of them had thought to bring a deck of cards. They'd all taken up smoking in Paris because it helped them execute their bad French, so it was necessary to open all of the windows in our two compartments. Through the bright, clearer air, past window sails snapping I noticed the stolid green and yellow fields and light blue and white country houses with their calming isolation. The lines of tall, ancient grass swayed like paper waves, and I could feel what it must be like in the fields at night when the owls came out to bless them.

There was the constant noise of the train and the piercing vigor of my classmates; I was glad to go to lunch in the quieter dining car. The people in our group had chosen each other and excluded others with relentless subtlety during the first week of classes. I sat with Rana of Jordan. She had dark brown eyes and only slightly lighter skin, and moved in a delicately erotic way. She asked me which of the guys I liked most, saying she had it in for Paul, who annoyed me by talking louder than everyone else and inserting English when he didn't know the French, which was often. ("Donnez-moi un card. Only un! J'ai un good hand – er – un bon hand!") Feeling pressed, I told her I thought Brian was cute.

That evening we arrived inside the brown walled fortress of Avignon, where I was given the address of a little apartment with a deep, perfectly square bathtub on the fourth floor of a five-story building on the river bed narrow Rue de Felix Gras, from the balcony of which I could just see the top of the Palais du Papes. Classes were held four times a week in a crudely cut, damp stone room two streets over from Felix Gras. Each Wednesday we had an excursion to a place near Avignon such as Arles, where Van Gogh had lived, or our literature professor's hometown of Fontaine de Vaucleuse, which had a nice windmill and the feel of the mountains.

By the first weekend it was Rana, Paul, Brian and I having pastisse as though we knew each other at L'Affiche, a jazz club.

"Be careful what you say to him, he doesn't care if you walk out of here with a crooked nose," I told Brian.

"You don't realize what he said about you, do you?"

"I'm not sure you know either."

"Like his drums are supposed to seduce you. Come on, let's get out of here."

"Where?"

"I don't know. He's so cocky."

The drummer of the jazz band looked a lot like Houdini.

I yelled to Rana and Paul as they came stumbling off the dance floor, "Brian wants to get going."

"Where you going, Brian?" Rana said.

"How about the Rio, by the school?"

"Yeah, the Rio's cool! That guy from Australia, the owner, he gave me a free beer just because I wasn't French!" Paul said.

"He's so cocky," Brian said again. I think he was drunker than I was, because I still thought everything was pretty funny.

"Forget about him, how can you be so bugged by some stranger? Is it the fact that he's French? Are you intimidated by French men?" I smiled and put a grape in his mouth. He looked off to the side as he chewed and swallowed with a tightness in his face, and I saw what it'd be like to be with him after the honeymoon was over.

The drummer didn't really look French and alerted my senses like deception does. He didn't look at me like he could have me, but like he was interested in having me. If I'd cut him off with a dirty look he would have looked away quickly and let the drums take over.

"Dancing is so wonderful, and Ass-staire here is such a good dancer," Rana was drunk, but still poised and flirting like a virgin.

I tried smiling at her.

"How you feeling, Marie? Let's go to the bathroom."

Rana put a wet towelette under her shirt and was smiling deep dark red. "So are we having a good time? I just love Paul. It's funny how quiet he gets. He's really sweet. He thinks we should go off by ourselves, but I'm not sure if I want to."

"Well, Brian's pissed off. The drummer came over and said something about how beautiful I was he'd like to eat me or something. I thought French people thought we were bad in bed."

"He's cute, you know. We could get rid of Brian for you."

"I wish I were French and could really talk to him. I'd just walk up, ask him if he'd like to have a drink down the street, and walk out."

"What, is Brian getting on your nerves really?"

"Yeah, why's he act like that ... we barely even know one another."

Neither of us went to the toilet and after we'd rinsed our hands and run them through our hair, we went back out. Rana had wonderful hair; brown, full and short, and beautiful, full lips. Paul didn't seem to care that the whole rest of the band had been looking at her.

With one final disgusted look at the drummer, Brian did pay the bill, like a true gentleman, and we went out into the late evening. I'd been careful not to step in any dog crap all night because it really was everywhere. The air was so warm that it smelled the way it does in summer at dusk in Oregon. We had all gotten some color in Antibes and I felt healthy. Beer didn't sound good as we walked by the little store that sold yellow custard that came preserved in a small paper container lined with plastic. It was the best thing I had ever eaten and having it right then sounded better than drinking.

Brian was holding my hand as I looked up at the black sky and saw nothing. No moon, no stars. The street was small and rough with pebbles and his shoes made a nice sound against them, like a horse's. "Careful," he was watching the crap for me while I looked up and wondered why they'd come. They had all been to France before and it seemed that they were ceramic and had simply been placed there as salt and pepper shakers on a table and would remain as they were when they came. They still saw French people as romantic excerpts depicted on black and white postcards rushing through the rain with baguettes, holding news-papers over their heads, and never thought that sometimes when they got home they sat on the couch for a long time in the late afternoon when rooms darken without turning any lights on.

Though it had only been a few seconds, I felt like I had been quiet a long time.

"Bougie ... bougie ... bougie!" Rana was saying in a childish voice.

"Stop it!" Brian pushed her further into Paul.

"What's your least favorite French word?" she asked me.

"I wish I knew my heritage better," I said.

Paul stopped dramatically to turn and look at me with his long, clownish face, flat blond hair and pale blue linen shirt. "Random!" He raised his hands in the air and shook them.

"That didn't answer the question, dahling," Rana said as she pulled on Paul and we started walking again.

"I'm gonna get drunk and go to class tomorrow," Paul said.

Brian smiled at me. "Pretend you're French for now."

The Rio was full and a guy who I knew to be a stunt man was drinking a light beer, which I thought was funny. He'd been in there the other two times I'd been in and had told me about how

61

he had worked with Gerard Depardieu. He wore a tight pink faux torn muscle shirt and had long, curly blond hair.

"Hey Joe, one beer and one gin, and what else?" Brian ordered for Rana. Rana always ordered gin.

"Wine wine wine," said Rana.

"And three wines."

"No, silly, Paul will have a straight shot of beer," she said.

"I don't want wine, either," I said. "I'll have vodka."

Rana was acting more drunk than she could have been, so we went upstairs to what was known at our school as the flirting room. We sat on the square cushions in the small carved out area to the left that faced the main room. The room felt very small, even with the mirrors on three walls, and the walls were velvet-colored, with one perfectly square window opened and held at a thirty-degree angle by a hook and chain. It let in the warm air, and caused all the trails of smoke to form twisted designs and pathways that ventually led to the outside world.

"My, this is good. It's really good and I know about gin, you know why? My dad raises it."

"How do you raise gin, Rana?" Paul was acting frattish and putting his hand all over her knee.

"Just like you raise your glass, like this."

"To what?" I asked.

"To our short vacation," Brian said.

"It's like taking a vacance from a vacation," said Paul.

"Only because you don't care about learning French," Brian said.

"Oh yeah, ca va monsieur cool guy, je voudrais un peu de respect s'il vous plait."

"Please, not so formal!" Brian said, smiling.

Paul didn't get it.

"La grammaire de Paul est tres superieuse," Rana said as sincerely as she could.

"Very funny," he said. "Tres blague, tres blague." He raised his glass and drank a lot of what was in it.

The French girls in the room all had long brown hair that fell gentle and straight and shook like tassels, and about half of them were talking to young French men. There were two other Americans in the room, both men, and it was their beards that kept them from getting women. The room was getting packed as three French boys came in and had to stand against the wall.

"Look at that girl over there," said Brian. "She's looking at us like we're not supposed to be here … it's an Australian bar, honey!"

"She's used to acting like that. All French women are bitches."

"Paul! You scary thing," said Rana.

"Everyone knows it."

"Are you drunk?" Brian asked me.

"Are you Australian?"

He just looked at me like he was tired of it.

"Are you drunk?" I was.

"Not really sure," he smiled, "I think it's been too long to tell."

"Just keep drinking then, until you're sure."

"What on earth are you two talking about?" said Rana.

"How tan Brian is."

"Dull." She drew it out. "Would you accompany me to the bathroom, dahling?"

"Not right now, please."

"I really can't hold my liquor."

"I don't have to go."

"Maybe she needs help," said Paul.

"Why don't you go help her, the bathrooms are coed anyway."

"I always forget that!" He had a nice, huge smile.

Rana stood up and sat back down. "That's good gin, I told you."

I whispered to Brian that she'd probably throw up in front of him, possibly even on him. He whispered back that he'd like whatever she did to him.

"You think he likes her that much?" I said after they were gone.

"He'd do anything."

"Well, yeah, to do it."

"What do you mean 'to do it'? What are you, five? No, I think he really likes her."

"Well, that's nice of him." I was getting sick of being with a smart frat boy. "Want another drink?"

"Yeah, what do you want?"

"No, I'll get it." I didn't even give him a chance to get his gentil ass up. The stairs were steep and narrow and I could hear Paul talking and Rana giggling in the bathroom next to the landing. As I was taking the first step down I saw someone turn in at the bottom. It was the drummer. He didn't wait for me to come down and I didn't wait for him either, even though it was obvious that there wasn't enough room for us to pass each other on the stairs. We met in the middle and he said, "Bon soir, such a nice evening, isn't it?"

"Oui, c'est encore chaud." His skin was coarse looking, like freshly rolled wheat dough. He was smiling and I looked at him and he looked at my mouth. I kept it frozen in this pose that I thought might be nice to look at, but eventually bit my bottom lip and asked him what he wanted to do. I said:

"Comment est-ce que tu desires faire ca?" which is the most elementary way of saying, 'How do you want to do this?'

"Comme ca." He took my hand and we went down the stairs and right through the corridor of the bar and out the door. It was a lot warmer than I'd wanted to admit to myself, because warmth makes me feel good, but lonely sometimes. Sometimes being there was so overwhelming that I didn't want to upset it and the warmth made it worse. I wished we were in Paris because small towns even in France can feel trashy but not in that seedy glamourous way. In the country it's more like a carnival. The purity is sacrificed to showmanship and the clean air makes the morning all the more painful in its lonely wasted loveliness.

"Tu es jolie, mais Americaine ..."

Mais Americaine; I laughed. He took it for granted that I understood things. "Oui, je suis un tramp Americain."

"Qu'est-ce que c'est qu'un 'tramp'?"

"Whore."

"Oh, non." He stopped to look at me, then kissed me. It was very nice. He had straight brown hair that fell around his eyes like a show curtain.

"Est-ce que tu veux voyager a Paris?" I said.

"Oui, jolie fille." He was speaking slowly. "Quand est-ce que tu veux y aller?"

"Maintenant."

"Ca va. Tu es folle?" He asked me if I were crazy.

"Oui."

"C'est bien ca. C'est un bon idee d'etre fou."

"Oui oui."

"Oui," he looked right at me again. He cared nothing about my friends. He was trying not to smile to hide any eagerness he must have felt.

He laughed as we walked by a brightly lit bar whose light and free feeling lit the sidewalk and crowd of singers in front of it. Their clamor was so elegant it sounded almost like a siren as they swayed together. But soon we'd be in the Montmartre, where the drunk outnumber the sober twenty to one and the theme of the neighborhood is dripping and scheming and saying you're sorry when you want to go home.

The train was not full, and it felt more empty than it was, especially in the club car. Around two a.m. as it was pulling slowly over the barrier between the countryside and the city I began to think. It is always a mistake to think while you're coming out of drunkenness. We'd had a few drinks on the way to the station, and on the train we'd had several more until I felt I might pass out. I knew I could get really drunk again in Paris and had excused myself from the café to go sit in a compartment nearby with a man from North Africa who gave me a piece of sticky fruit which he cut up with a knife from which he took pieces. I hadn't drunk steadily enough and it gave the eventual seemingly lucid illusion of having drunk nothing at all. Houdini was strong and could hurt me, I thought, though he seemed alright and comfortable to be around, but I was also no longer attracted to him. He'd been a drummer all his life, wasn't educated but read a lot, and was thirty-eight. If I did sleep with him I would have to be careful. I knew him now. There was nothing in it for me anymore. I thought of how I would have felt in the middle of the night and remembered when I used to be able to pass out and wake up clean. Now I hardly ever slept through the night and in the morning I knew I hadn't slept but had only come to. I would have left him in the bed of a ragged hotel on an obsolete floor at five thirty when everything everywhere is gray, even in America, and the only romantic part about it would have been how I had left him and walked through Paris just before it began to get light and gotten my ticket and gone to get an apple pastry just as it was getting light, and ridden the train back alone with the clammy hot feeling of too much so never enough until I was back in bed at my little apartment on Rue de Felix Gras with secrets to tell and a pissed off Brian who was no less of a fine guy for being such a jerk. I thought it was all better than going to bed early but it was a long trip and I was very tired.

I went to the back of the train and watched for the station. The lights came up confidently and clearly as those of an official place, but with the promise too of relief, like reaching home after a walk in the snow. I jumped off as Houdini was eating his last few pieces of ice. He lived near Paris anyway. His friends would bring his drums. I knew he'd wait for me a long time so I went and bought a ticket for the five o'clock to Avignon and walked out of the station.

It is very pleasant in Paris always because even when it has been raining and raining and raining you know that the rain has done something. To the city and to the people there. It was a fine mist of rain that night as I crossed one of the many small and beautiful bridges to an odd creperie and sat and watched the old man in the back drinking his café and reading a book after he had made me something to eat, and I drank coffee and ate the spinach crepe and wondered why he stayed open all night. I've heard that old people don't need as much sleep and I wondered if he missed it. His wife was probably gone and he was enjoying something like I was watching him, only he had learned to do it alone.

I sat drinking the café he had taken from the large bronze espresso machine and turned away from the old man reading to see, in a moment, a couple walking by looking very picturesque in their dark green raincoats. If they had looked in they would have seen a young woman at a small square table alone surrounded by other empty tables and the paintings on the walls. If either of them were very observant and had glanced far back enough they would have seen the counter drawn straight across and the large bronze espresso machine, but would doubtless have missed the blurry old man sitting just beyond it reading with a little white cup etched around his forefinger. They didn't look up, though, because they were together and arm in arm and very happy for the immediacy the rain brought to their relationship. I thought they were probably going home to make love and was jealous but I had the old man and he had had what they had but now he hadn't and was an old man and was I an old man – no, I wasn't, not like him because I hadn't had it yet and the thought made me apprehensive and I knew then that he missed it and that that was why he stayed open all night. I knew also that I was probably all wrong and that all the couple had was a walk in the rain and that he was just an old man who hated his wife and that I had drunk much too much and was, first and foremost, a student in a foreign country.

100 Years From Now

I have only ever heard my mother call one man "Sir." I call him Capt. Edie, and the only person who calls him by his first name is his wife. He is a doctor. But mostly he is one who never stands on ceremony. Ten years ago he told my mother she had to quit drinking before it killed her. They sat at his kitchen table and he looked across and told her, "No more beer." My mother is a writer.

Out back of his house now he cooks two steaks, one medium, one rare. The flames sear through the meat, turning its blood brown. I think it smells good even though I won't eat it. Mrs. Edie has been vegetarian for 25 years.

"Did you graduate yet?" he asks me.

"Magna Cum Laude."

"Good. Good. ... Your health good?"

"Yes, Captain. Except I finally got the chicken pox last year. That was bad. They had to give me pills to stop them coming."

"I had a surgery last year. The doctor asked me when I'd had my coronary bypass. I never had one. I had a coronary without knowing it. My blood pressure's good now. I hope to get ten years more out of life. ... I know that's nothing to you."

I looked at him, not wanting to disagree. "Ten years is a long time."

"I have to get this perfect for her." He turns the steaks another time and when he takes his off the flames go all the way down.

Their house has many things in it. Collections from when Mrs. Edie shut her gallery down and things brought home from Japan and Europe. Many things make squares; tables, paintings, sets of things. Capt. Edie has a collection of 25 muskets from more than one war. They are made of metal and wood designed as simple as death. They hang on the wall safely, in a hallway filled with painting supplies. In his bedroom is a cabinet full of scrimshawed whaling tools made of ivory.

Mrs. Edie brings vegetables and bread to the table as we sit. Capt. Edie holds a curiously large pepper mill above his meat. He pushes the top and we look over, responding to a sound like a battery-operated battle toy.

"What the expletive is that?"

"It's a pepper mill."

"It lights up."

"It was a gift."

"It's heavy."

"They're fancy people, the Morrisons."

"Must be the batteries."

"You have another book coming out?" Capt. Edie says to my mother.

"It's due in six months and she only has eighty pages!" I'm trying to be light, or carefree. It's just something I throw out there. A light gibe, maybe. I never teased my mom about anything.

"Miss, in a hundred years it's not going to matter if she starts today, next month or next year!"

But it would if she'd never started the book or never finishes it, I think.

"How is your steak?"

"Terrific."

"If it's too rare we can put it back on, the coals will be hot almost an hour."

"It's great, Sir."

"You should never sign a contract until you've finished, then you know it's yours," he says.

When I was eight, Capt. Edie gave me a scrimshawed ivory bodkin made into a necklace with four-pound test.

Tonight I lie on their couch under heavy blankets to fend off the severe air conditioning wondering what it will be like a hundred years from now and which things will matter and which won't. It seems someone will keep the scrimshaw and the muskets, as they are already so old.

The Root Cellar

Maren had observed him like a ghost. She knew he still allowed himself to listen to John Coltrane and drink scotch after work and into the evening, even though he'd told himself he wouldn't and would ride his bike after work instead. At least it kept him from thinking about her too much. His fear of alcohol dependence was a small price to pay. He had gotten the apartment while he was studying for the bar. She had nodded to herself when she saw it; it was much like the one he'd had his first year of law school – white, sterile, uncomplicated by history. Within his comfort zone. He set up the calfskin chair and ottoman his grandfather had given him next to the wall of windows. He termed this his "command center," after his father's home office. His father was a tall, facetious assistant vice president of customer relations, always a little too fat and self-satisfied to make it all the way up. Marc bragged that his father had once been considered a potential nominee for California governor, knowing deep down that it had been a shot in the dark, something an assistant chief-of-staff had thrown out at a cocktail party and no one had taken seriously, except in a fraternity frame of mind. "Yeah, Bud, go for it! I can see that face on yard signs ... you're better looking than the Governator!"

His father had had a heart attack four months earlier. His grandfather had died of a heart attack at 61, and he knew it wouldn't be too much longer for his father. His mother had she and his father on Weight Watchers and tried her best with her limited knowledge of what was healthy to keep him fit. But he snuck cheap beer onto their sailboat every other weekend, skiffing around the bay by himself. He was a man of almost no real ambition, but with enough respect for pampering to keep up the appearance of having some in order to get paid. Marc had never stood up to his father, or even refused a can of Bud from the doughy hand of the man he had lied to since he could talk. He remembered his father asking him about his dreams when he was little, because he was on ADD medication and nightmares were a side effect, and he'd told him he had dreams of sailing when he had actually dreamed of snakes piling on top of him, slithering around his room and into, and out of, his orifices.

Marc came out of the shower, the start of a Saturday with no agenda except to review some documents for Monday, which could wait until Sunday. He liked waiting until the last minute sometimes, just to be rebellious. He sat in front of a chocolate croissant and coffee. He looked down at them sitting on a plate and saucer, respectively, on the bamboo mat, then out the window across the room. From that angle all he could see was the building across the street, but from the command center chair, he could see the river. It was finally the beginning of summer, but this didn't matter to him much. He would go hiking by himself, or bicycling with Real from work, a skinny fifty-two year old with nothing to offer in the way of conversation except Wall Street Journal article summaries and recaps of the two trials he'd had that year.

He looked at his bookshelf. On the bottom was Maren's copy of Tender is the Night. He hadn't been able to get rid of it, and realized that he always thought of how it was there, trying to hide on the bottom shelf, but never acknowledged it. He thought about them watching Five Easy Pieces and making out on the couch the summer before; so thin and beautiful her little body had been in his big lap, and making love with her in the warm night in the little house they'd shared in law school that was like a farm house, and suddenly wanted a cigarette. He had one in a plastic bag that he'd saved from law school, his emergency cigarette for exams that he had never smoked because he'd had her to call instead.

He remembered the night of the Christmas party, afterward sleeping alone in the room with no curtains, curled up waiting for someone to tell him what to do.

"Oh my goodness!" she had said, smiling and starting to traipse across the back lawn of his new boss' house in Beaverton, the lawn dewing over in the late night cold. "That was the dullest thing ever ... an insult to the word 'party!'"

She'd looked over at his face, stern as she'd stopped in front of the car door, waiting for him to open it, her expression falling into disappointment like a child being reproached after thinking they'd done well in the Christmas play. They had gotten into the car as at dawn when people don't talk out of respect for others' sleepiness. Onto the cold suburban road they had driven, it reminding her of long drives she had taken alone in college, watching the silhouettes of the hills around Corvallis fold out onto each other, thinking of home.

She had grown up outside of Sullivan, New Hampshire, on 20 acres. She had told him about the deep yellow Banny eggs that were almost all yolk and the wild turkeys running out of the forest and hanging out with the chickens in the sometimes dusty, sometimes muddy clearing between the chicken house and the pond. What she missed most, she had said, were the cool evening frog songs that would come up from the bordering forest that hid a little bog about the same time as the fireflies started blinking on and off like little lit up potato bugs while she and her brother hit the last few volleys across the badminton net. This hadn't struck a chord with him until he'd hung out with her the summer of their third year of law school when they had lit candles in the back yard of their little farm house and he had felt the summer evening come on strong like it had never existed before.

After the "party" at his firm, he had floated through a red light without realizing it, and turned into a strip mall. The grocery store in it had still been open. He had parked as far away from it as possible; so far away that she had wondered where he was going when he got out of the car. She had sat there watching him walk – he always looked heavy when he walked, being so tall and thick and dressed in clothes that didn't fit him well.

She had gotten out and walked after him at the pace he was going, watching him enter through the automatic doors as though through a portal. He had wandered down a fruit and vegetable corridor and over to the side aisle, stopping in front of the pomegranate juice to stare at it. She'd come to stand beside him in line.

"Is there anything else we need?" he had asked.

She'd thought of several things. "No, I don't think so."

In the car his body had felt heavy as though he had gone swimming in his clothes, and he had not turned the key right away.

"What's wrong?" she had said, having known how futile the question was.

"I'm not like those people, they weren't even talking to each other. Where were they? Did you see the flowers; silk roses! in the bathroom?"

She had been relieved, until she 'd realized she couldn't respond honestly without pissing him off, because she knew he'd take the job anyway.

"You don't have to talk to them, they don't have to be your friends," she had said, even though she hadn't been able to imagine working every day with people who had spent three years studying to end up defending insurance companies and seeming fine with it, and who even alcohol didn't make interesting.

She'd thought about the young man he had told her about, pre-law-school Marc who had had a habit of going after work to have a drink at Smyth's bar around the corner from his tiny apartment in Manhattan, then had sat on the roof reading J. M. Coatzee (which she'd known was a problem, but had blamed it on immaturity, his lack of experience), watching the neighbors barbecue and feeling a foreigner. This was the man she had wanted to love, not the checked-shirt insurance pinch-hitter sitting next to her in the Volvo. But then again, he had also been a paralegal in Manhattan, and before that had worked for Wendell Wilke in D.C. He had been turning his clock key in the wrong direction maybe always. And his parents, a mother who kept his room exactly the same, down to the little twin bed not made for bringing anyone home and the model sailboat and the blue walls, and his father, the might-as-well-be an insurance adjuster or shoe salesman who had a speaker in his pillow piping classical music to help him sleep.

"Let's go," she'd said.

He looked at his Blackberry. Her number was still in there. He felt a wave of happiness as he thought of hearing her voice. He looked out the window at the Steel Bridge, black and harshly industrial, reminding him of nothing but the black-faced coal miners he'd seen on the cover of a book at Powell's earlier that week, no relation to the Steel Bridge, only just as professionally removed from him as those who'd built it.

After a while reading David Foster Wallace in the command center, he got in his car and drove, wound his way around the Columbia to a trail he'd found in a book and hiked until he almost passed out, stopping to sit on a log to eat red beans from a can and wanting to cry but not allowing himself to, fearing this would be the beginning of the end and he would end up moving to Hood River and opening a motel.

After work on Monday he felt a little satisfaction at turning in a brief he'd been working on since the week before. He walked two blocks over from the big pink reflecting pool of a building where he worked to Mary's Club and sat in the corner drinking scotch and thinking of her body in the flashing light of the credits of Venus, and her smiling in the tall grass on the top of Mt. Pisgah. They had hiked the gentle hill that was a mountain in Eugene together at least once a week after classes, taking the thin trails through the grass, sometimes sitting in it, he in his big straw hat. He had told her about his grandfather who had been fond of wandering, sometimes walking into the forest on family trips in the valley, not to return for hours.

He watched the young blond woman in front of him dancing topless for twenty minutes, then went home and sat by the window in his white apartment with the big black bird Picasso and the Deibenkorn he didn't even like until it was time to masturbate and fall asleep counting backward from a thousand, just to be sure.

In the morning he felt like he had melted into the bed and couldn't move. It was cold on the verge of raining outside his white down comforter – the window was open. It was grey inside and out. He decided to take a personal day and called his assistant. He thought of her right after he got off the phone.

They'd gone to Bend to wade in the river and he'd asked her if she wanted to live there after law school. He had always said things, just to see what they felt like. He didn't really mean them, but she took them to heart. She wanted to live in Bend, have a big garden and a root cellar, can jam and sell it at the Christmas market.

"Real life isn't like law school," he'd said. "But that's the cool thing about Portland, we can have those things there, too. I can't start my career in Bend."

She'd gotten a job at the courthouse as a clerk while he studied for the bar. They'd gotten an apartment together initially, until she'd gotten tired of feeling like she was becoming obsolete.

He put on some running shorts and his grey Princeton t-shirt and walked over to the Multnomah County courthouse where she worked. He sat on one of the benches next to the elk fountain, across from a man with a miner's beard who was smoking with ruddy yellowish fingers, and swaying. He felt this man knew something. He felt that this man, more than any other, could give him advice. He looked up to see Maren walking up Madison Street toward the courthouse. He watched her, a field mouse, walk across Fourth Avenue. He ran across the park and caught up to her.

"Marc," she looked horrified, but she was not surprised.

"Hi!" he smiled big and intensely as he had not done since his father had given him a stuffed elephant for passing preschool.

"Hi."

"How are you?"

"I'm okay."

"Good. Listen, come have coffee with me."

"We have a hearing at 8:30."

"I want to move to Bend."

"Good for you."

"Bend ..." he waited for it to sink in. "Let's move to Bend."

"What?" she smiled like someone had just fed her silicone pudding.

"I want to move to Bend with you."

"I'm seeing someone," she lied.

"Who is he? Is he a lawyer? Do I know him?"

"He makes bikes."

"Nice. He makes bikes."

"It's none of your business."

He looked at her. His eyes looked like they were made of buttons.

"Law school was a mistake for me. I hate working here. I thought you wanted to be a big corporate lawyer, your dream of living in the West Hills ... I thought you had to live in a city," she said.

He looked at her. She was so pretty. She had her mother's Native American cheekbones.

"I don't care about that as much anymore."

79

"You wouldn't be happy without your career. Even though I never understood how doing insurance defense would help you become a corporate lawyer. There aren't any corporate lawyers in Portland, and if there are, they're all very, very old." She missed him for a second. She remembered sitting in the park across from him by their house in law school where they would meet during lunch or after classes. His face had reminded her of a pencil tracing, delicate, like Rimbaud's. He had been so willing to lean back into the grass and just sit there. He had said, "I like being quiet with you."

He felt old. He felt very, very old. He couldn't walk away, but he did. He kissed her on the cheek in his mind and walked down the sidewalk back over to the strip of mostly empty benches. He glanced at the miner, still smoking and swaying into the distance. "I don't need a root cellar," he said under his breath as he passed the older, dark-suited attorneys and their youthful colleagues in bright unmatching shirts and ties on their way to morning call. He wandered toward Pioneer Square, feeling comforted by the ornate buildings he knew had been designed by A.E. Doyle, comforted by the Williams & Sonoma bowls he recognized from his mother's kitchen in their display window. He thought of Christmas with his family socked in at the beach near the artichoke fields, little trips, packages of bliss that pockmarked his now unchecked flat-lining trajectory.

Rimbaud had been a sailor, he remembered; he had sailed to Africa to trade slaves. Maren had never been able to reconcile the boy who had written the most beautiful poetry she had ever read with the man who had participated in the taking of the most beautiful thing that existed.

The Smallest of Entryways

She had her head cocked like a winter bud. The green faded tile floor with flecks of red, green, yellow color squares is much lower and me sliding around on it like drips of condensation down her window glass. The pots and pans, in and out of the cupboard, Lila's Brussels sprout seeds sprouting on the windowsill with the quiet light breaking in in the morning before we wake up and staying there until I go into the puce living room to cut paper. Lila why are you so rough with the delicate antique flower thin China like a W. Whitman hillside? You take them from their stacks or do some such while I take the pans out and look at the metal vent, sliding on the big pot, the one for black-eyed peas and spaghetti. You don't want me in there, but you do. You want me to see. To see you make bread, to see you mix the yeast in the flour, to see your effort. Edward doesn't care. He won't even give you money for a coat, but he buys coffee. He's better than you, he thinks because he didn't have me. You had me to see. At least you gave me the kitchen. A whole shelf above the stove. Spices. You are an artist, Mama.

Black marks floating notes very much more than I could ever ask for when I'm alone. Thank you for giving me the option to diffuse into my room and into yours like the smell of a growing leaf. You sit outside my room, on the couch but that isn't that far from my room and you listen. I didn't notice because of how happy I am. You go into the kitchen and you start typing. You shouldn't be typing while I'm on the flute. It's disruptive and you only type when I'm home. I think you don't do much of anything when we're not home. I think you watch "Guiding Light." I know you watch it because I've watched it with you when I had the flu. You know what's going on, I can tell.

The only thing at all like the kitchen is the garden. There are the stairs that then were good and the white trellis, all of these things donated you could say by the old pair who lived here before us. Squatting and dropping seeds – plip, plop, plip – into the divots in the rows like cake batter, little beans and tiny melons dna-ed and happy to begin. The fence was nice back then and the honeysuckle bush I would run to like a comet.

At the Lincoln Log school the kids said push it push the snow in huge plow like fashion with their tiny red and white mittens over by the cannons at the park, and even then I stayed behind with the teacher because it was warm and I didn't have to do anything. Taking off their wet things slick with melted snow bragging like Montessori kids. Picking my nose in the song circle. Nobody noticed until the teacher said, stop that it's not clean. There are piles of garbage on my bed. I can only use one cup or I get yelled at: "Use the same cup!" There are moth larvae crawling on my ceiling. I listen to Van Morrison and Peter Tosh before bed to drown out the typing and yelling. A Cricket in Times Square and later a cigarette in the dark and a Hershey's Chocolate tin with a nice old-fashioned girl as an ashtray.

The table is very big and the circle is easy to cut. At the next station there are fractions. Emily, my friend with the bowl cut tried to swallow her tongue and now her mouth sounds full when she talks. She turned her back and I colored Nebraska yellow and she got very upset. I helped my friend/crush Alexander tie his shoe. They only let me skip one grade because we came back from the island. It wouldn't have mattered if I'd graduated then. The horseshoe crabs taught me everything.

Edward wasn't there and then he was there hiking and playing baseball and telling me that my socks smelled like cat pee before we went to Herfy Burger with the cow head plastic bust over the entrance like he and Lila and I used to. Lila and Mary and Michael and I shopped at Prairie Market. This was before Winchell's was there even and before the first store I went to with bar codes lost their last cash register with any sense of itself. Gum was the first to go, then canned stuff and later cooler items and even finally bulk foods. Nothing was dusty anymore. Edward became the bottom of some old brown stairs trapped near the university, tiny cakes on my plastic blue and white doll plates.

The July of my seventh year I tried to become part of the blackberry bushes that flanked the old garage we had never once used for anything, that remained shut like the cold room had, a science experiment, one of the many caves she set up just in case. I knew I could not do it, I couldn't walk into them and have them take me as I was, a tiny bird, a rush dweller, so I made do with gathering the blackberries into a bowl until Lila called me in, tidelike.

She poured sugar gently onto them and I went in and sat on the deep red brocade couch that had come with the house to listen to an old man tell the news. There were old men newsmen back then who you could not doubt. Dick was outside mowing the lawn. He had been in the front yard making a fool of himself with the electric mower cord and was in the side yard now with the bright yellow forsythia, which I had never liked even though I knew I should, but I did like it because Lila liked it.

I looked over at her through the doorway of the kitchen past the kitchen table in front of the stove and my mind filled in that she was stirring something slowly. I watched the old man with his white hair's mouth bob and the sound of the mower made it harder for a second or so to hear so I looked back over and saw Lila darting from the dish drainer to the kitchen table to slam a tall shiny knife through the tablecloth into its fibers. She ran past me to the edge of the front part of the living room and turned on the record player, apologizing to me but still insisting on putting on the LP "Cats." She turned it up louder than the mower, scuttled over to the bureau like the land crab I remember seeing in the parking lot of Tom Thumb the day Dick had gone in to sell his first vile of mace when he was a salesman in the Keys and starting singing "Memory." She was balling, bursting with song, ladling it out for certainly me, certainly Dick, and certainly the neighbors on either side to hear, crying as though I had just died, one would think, and I watched Les Charles, the anchorman, the old, stoic anchorman, went into his soul for a second through the TV glass, forgot my mom, meditated, as it were, up until Dick was there on the disgusting bamboo chair holding her, she resisting, but being the straightjacket she had ordered.

This morning, the morning before all memory, she is in bed in the living room, what the room became when she got too sick to get up anymore. On Saturdays I used to sit on the back of the brocade couch where I used to watch the Smurfs, the exact place where I got my first headache and experienced the relief of my first Tylenol, and watch all the cartoons I could think of with my mother cooking in the kitchen next to me, the windows open sometimes, often rain fogging up the windows and becoming a reason in of itself to love each other. This morning she isn't there and I am not, I got up late because I could feel her not awake, not "to," and I lay in bed wondering if there was some way to make the window in my room not feel like that, not feel sad, feel sunny again, feel like the window to the outside, not just another picture on the wall.

Lila had been cut apart from herself when she was still unable to dress, when Ada still called to her that her bath was ready. She had a porcelain face with dark doll hair and wore layered dresses until she was 15 when she got to choose boys shorts and blue Keds with no comments from her lanky Ford model mother who had gone to UCLA and her father, the cross-dresser doctor; there was nothing wrong with that.

Her mother, her. There was no talking, no reasoning, just the heights. Never descending because valleys were clouded by the eternal force in her glass, tinkling around everything. Never would you think such a delightful sound could be so sinister. Tiny Lila never had a moment to relax. Ada tended her like a horse but without blood to do those things there is something missing. The ones who shared it were all like her mother and that's what she became too, a pause, the sound in between beats that cocks your ears in anticipation, the breath before a laugh.

The thing that was most different about Lila was there was no tinkling or fancy dresses, except the Jessica McClintocks Big Mama's daughter would send that I would scale the metal fence in to grab a quick glass of milk or the h'ors d'oevres Lila would make for me and my friends. You can take the debutante out of the ball, but you can't take the ball out of the debutante, it seemed. Our house in the old city was damp and sombre with pictures torn from art books of the Virgin Mary and streaks of mutterings on the walls melted there by her eternal frying and boiling. After Edward left the island we headed for was small, the cabin was small, there were bunk beds and faux wood and the reason for the lack of tinkling was Lila drank beer from a can. Cockroaches crawled in, and everything absurd was funny. We were teenagers, all of us. But I only wanted to learn how to talk to the bunnies and land crabs and learn who all the fishes were and the great white heron who came to visit while I was fishing and Lila sunning on the little white rocks. I woke each day hoping and for years not even penetrated by the typing and the memories of tinkling and the deep imprint of sorrow in her face.

I don't like to talk about Dick. I feel he has been drawn badly by Lila and he had a hard start because he came into my room while I was being alone with my tornado cellar thoughts and I had to stand by the mirror while he asked me ceaselessly if I would simply respond to him, in any fashion, preferably hello. He became a part of her, washed asunder by her tide, only to surface through stories of Norway and the conquerors, and his quintessential childhood, an upbringing thrown off by beauty.

He was the umpire, then the tour guide, the sense of reason, then the other voice in the hallway outside the bathroom. The Easter Bunny tooth fairy and finally the man on the couch, waiting to be escorted out by a teenage girl who had never learned to respect adults lying to themselves (sense of decency). For years I went again to the small Fishing and Hunting publishing building where I would check on him, see the photograph of Lila covered in a fishing vest and know that he was ruined, grab 20 dollars and build on my growing sense of relief that I was not and would never be that, whatever it was, that carried the past around not only not so obviously but at all.

In the ancient summer day he held her like a rock in his hand until she went back into the kitchen to make gumbo. That tiny thread like the rope around a boat edge had been bitten off when she was a small puff of steam. Everything was painted that way.

The morning of I came into the living room where my mother lay sunken into the waterbed, Saltines and beer next to her, the bent 1960s blinds drawn to cover the daylight.

"Can I watch cartoons? The dishes are done. The Smurfs are on. Fat Albert is almost over ..."

She feigned sleep or at least a daze. I walked back into the kitchen. I looked for a moment at the neat array of dishes in the dish drainer, wondering if I had put them in there in the right order, as an adult might have done. I removed the step stool, placing it under the sink, leaving the white washed kitchen washed in bathing daylight, the green flecked tile floor remembering me, remembering me to myself, and went into my room to play the flute. I left the door open a crack that I might not be trapped within my own room, or have a garden without light or appetite.

CPSIA information can be obtained at www.ICGtesting.com
Printed in the USA
LVOW071948101212

311028LV00005B/37/P